D0261149

Grandpa's Car

by Sue Graves

Illustrated by Garyfallia Leftheri

First published in 2011 by
Franklin Watts
338 Euston Road
London
NW1 3BH

Franklin Watts Australia
Level 17/207 Kent Street
Sydney
NSW 2000

A CIP catalogue record for this book is available from the British Library.

ISBN 978 1 4451 0285 6 (hbk)
ISBN 978 1 4451 0291 7 (pbk)

Series Editor: Jackie Hamley
Editor: Melanie Palmer
Series Advisor: Catherine Glavina
Series Designer: Peter Scoulding

Printed in China

Franklin Watts is a division of
Hachette Children's Books,
an Hachette UK company.
www.hachette.co.uk

Alfie and Grandpa were going to the shops.

"Let's go on the bus,"
said Alfie.

"No let's go in my car,"
said Grandpa.
"I like my car better."

But Grandpa's car was old.

It was very old.

It went **bang**!

It went **whizz!**

It went

whizz

bang!

The car stopped.

“Oh dear!”
said Grandpa.
“What shall we do?”

“Let’s go on the bus,”
said Alfie.

"I like my car," said Grandpa. "But I like the bus better!"

Puzzle Time!

Put these pictures in the right order and tell the story!

surprised

scared

proud

worried

Which words describe Grandpa and which describe Alfie?

Turn over for answers!

Notes for adults

TADPOLES are structured to provide support for newly independent readers. The stories may also be used by adults for sharing with young children.

Starting to read alone can be daunting. **TADPOLES** help by providing visual support and repeating words and phrases. These books will both develop confidence and encourage reading and rereading for pleasure.

If you are reading this book with a child, here are a few suggestions:

1. Make reading fun! Choose a time to read when you and the child are relaxed and have time to share the story.
2. Talk about the story before you start reading. Look at the cover and the blurb. What might the story be about? Why might the child like it?
3. Encourage the child to retell the story, using the jumbled picture puzzle as a starting point. Extend vocabulary with the matching words to characters puzzle.
4. Give praise! Remember that small mistakes need not always be corrected.

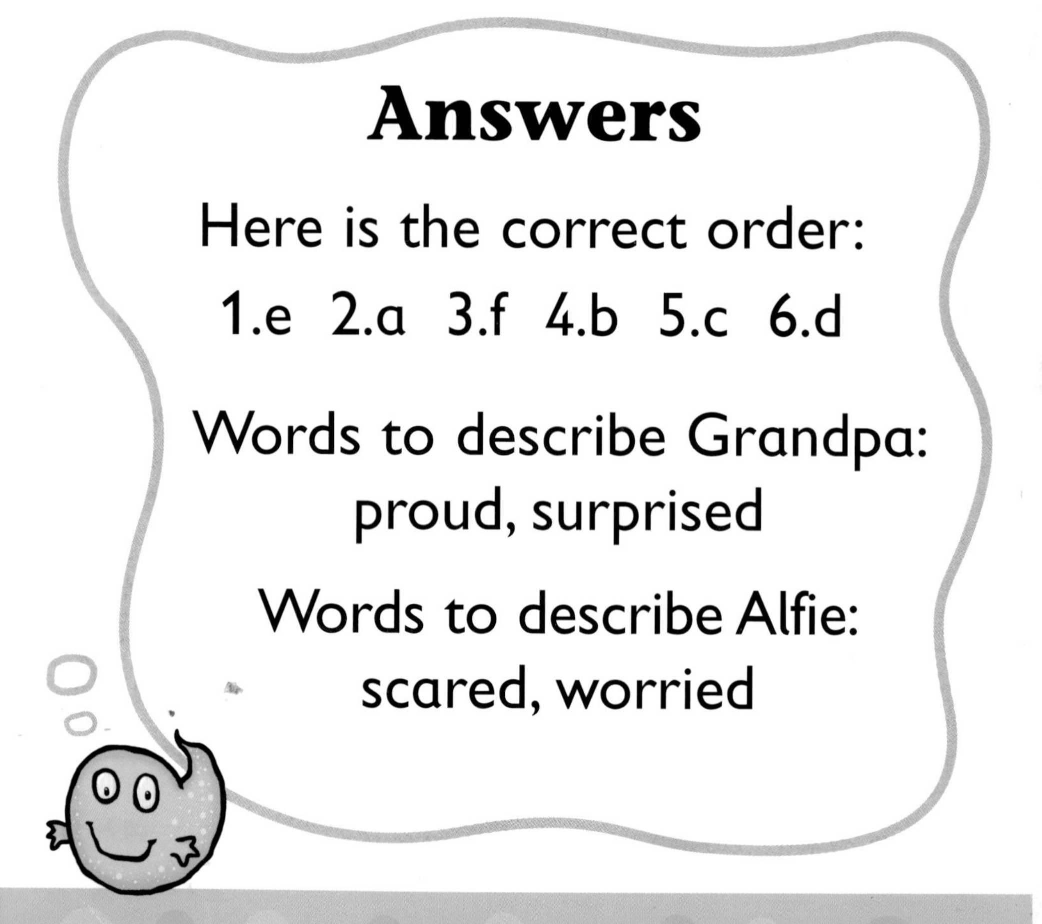

Answers

Here is the correct order:

1.e 2.a 3.f 4.b 5.c 6.d

Words to describe Grandpa:
proud, surprised

Words to describe Alfie:
scared, worried